DEAD
MEN'S
WATCHES

Also by Hugh Hood

NOVELS

White Figure, White Ground 1964
The Camera Always Lies 1967
A Game of Touch 1970
You Cant Get There from Here 1972
Five New Facts about Giorgione 1987

THE NEW AGE/LE NOUVEAU SIÈCLE

I: *The Swing in the Garden* 1975
II: *A New Athens* 1977
III: *Reservoir Ravine* 1979
IV: *Black and White Keys* 1982
V: *The Scenic Art* 1984
VI: *The Motor Boys in Ottawa* 1986
VII: *Tony's Book* 1988
VIII: *Property and Value* 1990
IX: *Be Sure to Close Your Eyes* 1993

STORIES

Flying a Red Kite 1962
Around the Mountain: Scenes from Montréal Life 1967
The Fruit Man, the Meat Man, and the Manager 1971
Dark Glasses 1976
Selected Stories 1978
None Genuine without This Signature 1980
August Nights 1985
A Short Walk in the Rain 1989
The Isolation Booth 1991
You'll Catch Your Death 1992

NONFICTION

Strength down Centre: The Jean Béliveau Story 1970
The Governor's Bridge Is Closed 1973
Scoring: Seymour Segal's Art of Hockey 1979
Trusting the Tale 1983
Unsupported Assertions 1991

The New Age/
Le Nouveau Siècle
X

DEAD MEN'S WATCHES

A NOVEL

HUGH HOOD

Published in 1995 by
House of Anansi Press Limited
1800 Steeles Avenue West
Concord, Ontario
L4K 2P3
Tel. (416) 445-3333
Fax (416) 445-5967

Canadian Cataloguing in Publication Data

Hood, Hugh, 1928–
Dead men's watches

(The new age; pt. 10)
ISBN 0-88784-168-6

I. Title.   II. Series: Hood, Hugh, 1928–
The new age; pt. 10.

PS8515.049D4 1995   C813'.54   C95-930018-X
PR9199.3.H66D4 1995

Cover Design: Bill Douglas/The Bang
Computer Graphics: Tannice Goddard, S.O. Networking
Printed and bound in Canada

*House of Anansi Press gratefully acknowledges the support of
the Canada Council, the Ontario Ministry of Culture,
Tourism, and Recreation, Ontario Arts Council, and
Ontario Publishing Centre in the development of
writing and publishing in Canada.*

*For Michael and Elizabeth Bliss
and their very handsome family
with my fondest admiration*